WHO'S A
CLEVER GIRL?

Crabtree Publishing Company

www.crabtreebooks.com

PMB 16A, 350 Fifth Avenue
Suite 3308
New York, NY 10118

612 Welland Avenue
St. Catharines, Ontario
Canada, L2M 5V6

Impey, Rose.
  Who's a clever girl? / Rose Impey ; illustrated by Andrâe Amstutz.
    p. cm. -- (Yellow bananas)
    Summary: Jake Juggins and his pirate band decide they need a girl on board
ship to do the chores while they are busy having daring adventures, but the girl
they choose has other ideas.
    ISBN 0-7787-0930-2 (RHC) -- ISBN 0-7787-0976-0 (pbk.)
    [1. Sex role--Fiction. 2. Pirates--Fiction. 3. Schools--Fiction. 4. Humorous sto-
ries.] I. Amstutz, Andrâe, ill. II. Title. III. Series.
PZ7.I1344 Wj 2003
[E]--dc21
                                        2002009544
                                        LC

Published by Crabtree Publishing in 2002
Published in 1999 by Egmont Children's Books Limited
Text copyright © Rose Impey 1985
Illustrations copyright © André Amstutz 1985
The Author and Illustrator have asserted their moral rights.
Reinforced Hardcover Binding ISBN 0-7787-0930-2 Paperback ISBN 0-7787-0976-0

1 2 3 4 5 6 7 8 9 0 Printed in Italy 0 9 8 7 6 5 4 3 2

Rose Impey

WHO'S A CLEVER GIRL?

Illustrated by
André Amstutz

who's a clever girl?

YELLOW BANANAS

1

The pirate crew

IF YOU THINK this is the kind of story where
five children, armed only with a bucket and
spade, catch a dangerous band of smugglers,
you'd be wrong. And if you think this is the
kind of story where a poor, helpless little girl is
captured by a terrible crew of cut-throat pirates
. . . you'd still be wrong, but a lot closer. Now,
those are all the hints I'm going to give you. To
find out what happens, you'd better read on . . .

Once upon a time, and not so very long ago, a little girl was walking to school. She was a sensible girl, who could pack her own lunch and do her mom's shopping without losing the change. She was also far too sensible to talk to strangers she met in the street, especially ones with peg legs, scars on their faces, patches over their eyes, and scruffy parrots on their shoulders. So when she saw four strange characters fitting this description, she quickly turned the other way and kept on walking.

But the pirates had seen her. She was just
what they were looking for.

"You look like a sensible girl," growled the
biggest pirate, who was called Jake. "We want
a sensible little girl like you to join our crew,
don't we, mateys?"

"Yes, yes," agreed the rest of the gang,
covering their mouths to hide their smiles.

"We're rough, tough pirates and we sail the
seas in a mighty, fine pirate ship. We have rare
adventures, don't we, mateys?" boasted Jake.

"Oh yeah, yeah," said the rest of the crew.

They didn't seem quite so sure about this.

"All we need is for you to join us, then we can go off on raids. Isn't that right, mateys?" said Jake.

"Yes! Yes!" they agreed, more strongly this time, again covering their mouths to hide their smiles.

Now the little girl knew better than to listen to this kind of story from such nasty-looking villains. She knew they were up to no good. But the idea of having an adventure was far too tempting to miss. She didn't exactly stop, but she walked on more slowly.

"Come on, what do you say? Har Har! It would be more fun than going to school, I'll wager," said Jake.

Well, the little girl couldn't argue with that, could she?

She stopped and stared into Jake's big, black eyes. "Would you really make me into a real pirate?"

"On my honor," swore Jake, trying hard to look honest.

"On my honor."

"Would you give me a real pirate outfit?"

"To be sure, my hearty," said Jake.

The other pirates stepped forward and gave her

a scarf

a belt

a hat

and a patch.

"What about a parrot?" she said.

For a moment Jake was stunned, but he settled the parrot on the little girl's shoulder.

"Shiver me timbers! You strike a hard bargain," he snarled. "Now, let's go. Back to the ship."

The little girl was pleased with herself. The pirates looked happy too. They thought they had tricked her. And, if you don't tell the little girl, I'll tell you why.

You see, these pirates were not too happy. They used to sail the seas in a battered ship called *The Leaky Tub*. And it did leak too. The pirates didn't mind, as long as it stayed afloat. Most of the time it did. Then one day they had a bit of luck. They attacked a handsome

galleon. The galleon crew just ran away and never came back. Jake and his men found themselves the proud owners of *The Flying Dragon*. That was when their problems started.

The ship proved to be a lot of work. It was big and shiny and it seemed a shame not to keep it clean. Jethro began to scrub and swab the decks. He polished the brass until he could see his face in it. The other pirates liked to see the ship sparkling. It made them feel proud.

There was a cook's galley, with pots and pans and kitchen tools. Joshua liked cooking. He made marvelous meals like seafood risotto, octopus in red wine and chilli sauce, prawn pancakes, and a wonderful ice cream dish with peaches and grapes and chocolate sauce.

There was also a cabin full of canvas and
sailcloth and needles and thread. Jem was good
at sewing. He could patch the sails and tack
and turn a seam. He made curtains and
cushions and soon the pirates had new outfits.
They enjoyed looking stylish.

Finally, there was a cozy captain's cabin, filled with maps and charts. Jake loved to sit in the captain's chair, with his foot up, planning and plotting routes and dreaming about finding buried treasure.

For a while the pirates were happy but soon Jake wanted some adventure. However, the others were always too busy, cleaning and cooking and mending.

"Jumping jelly!" Jake roared. "You're turning into a bunch of ship-wives. This isn't a rest-home for worn-out sailors. We're rough, tough pirates. We should be raiding and rampaging."

The pirates looked ashamed of themselves. But then they said:

"Who's going to cook the meals?"

"Who's going to keep the decks clean?"

"Who will do the making and mending?"

"Giant jam tarts! That's girl's work," snarled Jake. 'We'll get some gullible little girl to do those jobs, then we can have adventures."

And that is just what they did, as easy as that. Or so they thought, for they were old-fashioned pirates. They didn't realize that little girls are too clever to be caught that way. But don't worry, they're going to find out!

2

The Pirates Find Out

SO OFF THEY all went, down the road, through the alley, along the path, and toward the canal bank. The path ran along the bottom of the schoolyard. The pirates kept their heads down, but the little girl didn't. She would have loved her friends to see her, all dressed up. The pirates couldn't believe how smoothly it had all gone. They thought to themselves, "Are little girls really that easy to fool?"

When they reached the ship, Jake led the way up the gangplank.

"Welcome aboard *The Flying Dragon*," he said. The little girl was amazed by what she saw. Each of the pirates was impatient to show her what work she would have to do. The little girl was surprised to be so popular.

"Those pirates are up to something," she thought.

First, Jethro showed her the decks and cabins. He showed her the mops and buckets and the polish. He told her all she had to do.

"You better do a good job. I like to see my face in this brass."

The little girl was surprised. "I'm not doing the cleaning," she thought. "Whoever heard of pirates dusting and polishing?"

Next, Joshua took her to see the cook's galley

and showed her the pots and pans.

"We expect good food," he warned her. "No lumps in the potatoes, no soggy cabbage, no watery soup."

The little girl was even more surprised. "I'm not doing the cooking," she thought. "Whoever heard of pirates baking?"

Then Jem showed her the tailor's cabin. He showed her the needles and thread and rolls of material.

"We like to look stylish. We can't have holes in our clothes when we go on raids," he said.

The little girl began to look upset. "I'm not doing the mending," she thought. "Whoever heard of pirates sewing?"

She was looking for adventure, and she was determined to find it.

At last Jake showed her the captain's cabin. He showed her all his maps and charts. The little girl's eyes widened. Her fingers began to itch.

"Curdled Custard! Keep your female fingers off those charts!" he shouted. "You can come in here to flick a duster around, if you're careful, but don't touch anything. Plotting and planning is my job and you'd better keep out of my way."

Now the little girl was angry. She stared into Jake's big, black eyes.

"Did you really think I was going to join a pirate crew to do the cooking and the cleaning? Did you think I would fall for a trick like that? Girls don't have to do that kind of thing. Girls can have adventures just like boys." And to prove it she came up with her own clever plan.

The pirates were surprised and disappointed. If girls didn't do this kind of thing who was going to cook and clean and sew? It seemed they still had their problem after all. The little girl looked at their puzzled faces.

"Don't worry, I know how we can sort this out. We can have a vote. That way we all decide who should do each job," she said.

The pirates were completely confused. They had never come across this idea before. She tried to explain. "We vote for the person who is best for each job. Then, in the end, everyone will be happy."

"First," said the little girl, in her teacher's voice, "who makes delicious doughnuts, tasty treats, and perfect puddings? Who should do the cooking?"

The pirates began to feel hungry. They all turned to Joshua and pointed at him.

"Good," said the little girl. "Then that's decided and *everyone* is happy."

Joshua didn't look happy, he looked puzzled, but all the others were smiling. They didn't have to do the cooking.

"Now," said the little girl, "who can make the brass brightest and the decks dazzle? Who should do the cleaning?"

The pirates liked their ship clean. They all

turned to Jethro and pointed at him.

"Good," said the little girl, "then that's decided and *everyone* is happy."

Jethro didn't look happy, he looked puzzled, but all the others were smiling. They didn't have to do the cleaning.

"Next," said the little girl, "who can stitch a straight seam and patch a pair of pants? Who should do the sewing?"

The pirates were proud of their fine clothes. They all turned to Jem and pointed at him.

"Good," said the little girl, "then that's decided and *everyone* is happy."

Jem didn't look happy, he looked puzzled, but all the others were smiling. They didn't have to do the sewing.

"Finally," said the little girl, "we must choose the captain. This is an important job."

Jake was smiling. He liked being captain and giving orders. He enjoyed having plenty of time to plot and plan and dream about buried treasure.

But the little girl went on, "Who is the cleverest person on this ship? Who is best at telling other people what to do? Who is crafty and cunning and good at getting their own way? Who should be captain?"

All the others turned to Jake. He was certainly good at getting his own way. Then they looked at the little girl. She was far more clever and cunning than Jake. They all pointed at her.

"Good," said the little girl, "then that's decided and *everyone* is happy. You can be captain's mate," she said to Jake.

Jake wasn't happy, he was hopping mad, but what could he do?

"Now back to work you good-for-nothing land lubbers," she shouted, "and be quick about it."

The pirates disappeared to do their work and soon the ship set sail. *The Flying Dragon* glided along the canal bank until it came to a fork where it joined a wide river. Gathering speed, it sailed down the river until, as the sun was setting, it reached the open sea.

The little girl sat in the captain's chair with her feet on the captain's table. She couldn't believe how smoothly it had gone.

"Are pirates really that easy to fool?" she wondered.

3

Adventures at Sea

SOON THE LITTLE girl and Jake were busy
planning raids. They made attacks on other
ships, when they could tempt the crew away
from their cooking and cleaning. They scaled
the rigging. They manned the cannons.
They hoisted the sails and went in search
of adventure.

Their first victory was over a tough sea dog
called Captain Crackers. Some people said he

was 105 years old. You would never have guessed it to see him swing from the rigging with a knife between his teeth. But after he met the little girl he decided to retire.

Next, they got the better of the well-known villain, Captain Cut-throat.

"I'll slice you up and feed you to the sharks," he said. But things didn't work out like that. He was made to walk the plank, along with the rest of his crew.

Their greatest adventure was when they were attacked by a black-hearted pirate called Captain Bonnet. He and his scurvy crew came

aboard *The Flying Dragon* ready for action, but
the ship seemed to be deserted. Jake and his
men were hiding. They often did this when the
fighting got too fierce. The little girl had
climbed the tallest mast. She cut free a huge
sail which fell to the deck, trapping the
pirates underneath.

Now Jake and the pirates could see what little girls were made of.

After a while the pirates needed a rest. They wanted to get the place ship-shape again. But the little girl had a real taste for adventure now. She was preparing a new plan, to make a pirate raid on her school.

She would terrify the teachers and scare the secretary. She would capture the janitor and chase the children around the schoolyard. She would take the school by storm and force the principal to walk the plank! She was very excited about this plan.

But the other pirates were not too happy about it.

"Whoever heard of pirates attacking a school full of kids?" grumbled Jake, who was getting fed up with the little girl and her clever ideas.

"That's why it's such a good idea," said the little girl. "Because nobody would expect it. We have the element of surprise."

"But there would be nothing to steal. Who wants hundreds of rulers and pairs of rusty scissors?" said Jethro.

"Ah, but on Mondays there's a lot of money. It takes the secretary all morning to count it. I've seen her. Piles of it all over her desk."

The little girl wasn't really interested in the money, it was the glory she wanted, but she had to keep the pirates happy.

"There's only five of us. There must be hundreds of them," said Joshua.

"They don't count," said the little girl, who felt like a real pirate by now. "They're just a bunch of kids and a few teachers. They'd be no problem."

None of the pirates looked convinced. They thought it was a foolish idea. The little girl could see she had a problem. She changed her tactics.

"Okay, who is in charge around here? Who was chosen to be captain of this ship? Who makes the decisions?" she said.

All the pirates turned and pointed to her. They knew when they were beaten.

"Good," said the little girl. "Then that's decided and *everyone* is happy."

"Really," she thought. "Pirates are so gullible."

4

School Ahoy!

ON MONDAY MORNING, as the sun began to rise, *The Flying Dragon* left the open sea and sailed into the mouth of the wide river. Soon it reached the fork where the river joined the canal. It glided along the canal until, at last, the school came into view.

"School ahoy!" called the little girl. "Weigh anchors, mateys."

The pirates lowered the gang plank and left the ship. They crept across the schoolyard to the entrance. The little girl pushed the front door open and they all peered inside. It was 11 o'clock and the children had just come in from recess, so the school was very quiet. Every sound seemed to echo down the tiled hall.

The little girl felt nervous coming into school at this time. It was like having been at the dentist and coming back late, feeling strange and shy. But she found herself carried along by

School Ahoy!

the others. They just wanted to get it over with and get back to the ship. They felt uncomfortable on dry land.

In front of the gym a display of dinosaur models was gathering dust. Muddy footprints led all the way into the boys' locker room.

"What a mess," said Jethro. "Doesn't anyone keep this place clean?"

While the others were arguing about which direction to go, he took off his scarf and began to polish the brass handles on the doors.

"Oh yuck, I smell meatloaf and Brussels sprouts," said Joshua. He followed a terrible smell which drifted down the hall from the school cafeteria. Peeping through an open

classroom door, Jem could see a sewing class waiting patiently while the teacher threaded needles for a long line of children. He thought he would go in and give her a hand.

By the time the little girl and Jake entered the secretary's office they had lost the rest of the crew.

Miss Crow, the school secretary, was arranging an enormous heap of money into tidy piles and scribbling numbers into her ledger. She looked tired and irritable. She kept sighing and

scratching her head. They waited for her
to look up from her counting but she didn't.
Finally she spoke, "Put it down on the table,"
and then, "Thank you!"

When Jake moved forward at the sight of so much money, she snapped, "Keep those fat little fingers off the money." He jumped back in alarm, looking guiltily at his hands.

The little girl decided to take over, "We've come for the money," she said. Miss Crow was not impressed. She still didn't look up.

"Well it isn't ready yet," she said. "And don't use that tone with me. Really, I've only got two hands, you know. It's always the same on Mondays. Rush, rush, rush. I do the best I can and if it isn't good enough . . . well . . . I'm sorry but . . ."

The little girl and Jake backed out of the

secretary's office and closed the door quietly.
They both felt guilty.

"Shiver me timbers!" whispered Jake, and the
little girl nodded in agreement.

At that moment they heard a voice coming from the gym, which the little girl recognized. It was the voice of Mrs. Raven, the principal. She didn't sound happy either.

"No, no, no, that's hopeless," she said in a weary voice. "You're supposed to be fierce and bloodthirsty. You wouldn't scare a rabbit. If only we had some real pirates," she said, "then we might see some action."

At this, the little girl and Jake began to feel
better. They drew their pirate pistols and rushed
into the gym.

"Abandon ship, you miserable varmints, or
we'll string you from the flagpole," roared the
little girl. Children flew screaming in all
directions. Some of them hid behind Mrs. Raven.

The little girl looked at them. They were
children she knew and they were all wearing
pirate outfits. She felt cheated. She stared open-
mouthed at them while they stared back at her.
It wasn't fair. She was speechless.

But Mrs. Raven was delighted. "Oh, well
done, Mary Mansfield! That's more like it. We'll
find a part for you in our play." The children
were crowding around her and Mrs. Raven was

patting her on the back.

"That's what I wanted, children, a really bold pirate voice. You've got to sound like pirates, as well as look like them. Your . . . er . . . friend looks the part," she said politely, turning to Jake. "Perhaps you might be able to advise us on costumes, Mr . . . ?"

"Jake Juggins, at your service, your honor," said Jake, shaking hands roughly with the principal.

Seeing the little girl busy with her friends, he added, "Captain of *The Flying Dragon.*"

Mrs. Raven sent the children back to their classrooms. Then she explained to Jake that they were practicing for the Christmas play. They were doing Peter Pan. Mrs. Raven told Jake she was having problems with the pirates. Jake gave her a lot of advice. He told her what the pirates should wear and the kinds of things they should say.

A few of these ideas were not quite suitable, but Mrs Raven was too polite to say so.

At lunchtime the little girl went to look for the pirates. She found Joshua in the school cafeteria, helping serve the lunch. Jethro was telling the school janitor how to get a better shine on the gym floor. Jem was teaching two young boys to sew buttons on their coats.

Peeping through the office window, the little girl spotted Jake, who was now having a cup of tea with the principal. Mrs. Raven had a selection of maps and a large globe. There were countries marked on it that Jake had never even heard of.

Great Goulash

"Great goulash, your worship," said Jake, who had never met a principal before, "you run a splendid ship, if I may say so."

As for Mary Mansfield, she was happy to be back. She became the heroine of the school. She was glad she hadn't missed the play. She was bound to get the part of Captain Hook. All her friends wanted to hear about her adventures. She told them how she captured a gang of cut-throat pirates single-handed, became their captain, led raids on enemy ships, and collected enough treasure to sink a school. At last, when she got tired of that, she had tricked the pirates into bringing her home. And to prove it – here she was.

She discovered that telling the stories was nearly as good as having the adventures. She thought she might be a writer when she grew up. She already had a lot of ideas. She was, after all, a very clever little girl. But then, most girls are, in my experience.

# YELLOW BANANAS

Don't forget there's a whole bunch of Yellow Bananas to choose from: